The Little Girl with the Curl

Characters

Narrator

Sally

Mom

Dad

Teacher

Setting

Sally's home and school

Picture Words

Sight Words

go	no	now	to
up	was	what	yes

Enrichment Words

fix

time

very

wake

Narrator: Sally was sleeping late on a school day.

Sally: Zzzz . . .

Mom: Wake up, Sally.

Sally: Yes, Mom.

Dad: Make your bed, Sally.

Sally: Yes, Dad.

Narrator: In the morning, Sally was a good little girl.

Mom: Wash up, Sally.

Sally: Yes, Mom.

Mom: Fix your curl.

Sally: Yes, Mom.

Dad: Go to school now.

Sally: Yes, Dad.

Narrator: Sally was very good at school, too.

Teacher: What is 2 and 2?

Sally: 4.

Teacher: Very good, Sally!

Teacher: What is 3 and 3?

Sally: 6.

Teacher: Very good, Sally!

Narrator: But at bedtime, Sally was *not* a good girl. At bedtime, Sally was *bad*.

Mom: Wash up, Sally.

Sally: No.

Dad: Time for bed, Sally.

Sally: No!

Mom: Go to sleep, Sally.

Sally: NO!

Narrator: At bedtime, Sally was very bad. In fact, she was horrid!

Sally: No, no, no, no, no!

The End